Celebrate with the **MR. MEN** and **LITTLE MISS!**

MR. MEN
LITTLE MISS
Celebrations

www.mrmen.com

egmont.co.uk

£3.99

ISBN 978-1-4052-8879-8

9 781405 288798

KU-514-850

Would you like your **child** to **star** alongside the Mr Men in their very **own** story?

Every child will love reading about themselves sharing a very silly birthday in true Mr Men style!

"Now, that's what I call lucky," said Little Miss Lucky.

"Oh no!" cried Little Miss Neat. "However are we going to chase away next year's bad luck?"

"HELLO!" boomed a very loud voice, suddenly.

It was Mr Noisy.

And, as you know, Mr Noisy is very loud.

More than loud enough to scare away any bad luck.

Loud and red!

On the last day of the New Year celebrations, Little Miss Neat invited all her friends round to her garden. She had bought lots of fireworks because the loud bangs would chase away all the bad luck for the next year.

But she had not counted on Mr Bump.

Mr Bump is not a very lucky person.

In fact, he is not lucky at all.

While he was carrying the fireworks, he somehow or other managed to trip and he somehow or other managed to drop all the fireworks into the pond.

After this everyone gave each other a red envelope with a gift of money inside.

Everyone?

Well, not quite everyone.

Every time Mr Mean tried to give away his red envelope he just could not quite bring himself to do it.

He truly is the meanest man in the world!

The next day Mr Muddle led the Dragon dance down the street.

Unfortunately, what followed Mr Muddle's lead …

She was so embarrassed she turned bright red.

"You'll have luck all year," laughed Little Miss Lucky.

Each New Year was represented by a different animal.

There were twelve animals and Little Miss Naughty was born in the year of the Rat.

After dinner, she crept up behind Little Miss Shy wearing a rat mask.

Little Miss Shy screamed and leapt in the air.

He even ate all the fish!

Little Miss Neat was not very happy because it was a Chinese New Year's custom to leave some of the fish.

Greedy old Mr Greedy!

Everyone was very excited when they arrived for New Year's Eve dinner that evening.

It was an enormous feast.

Mr Greedy grinned in pleasure and tucked in.

He ate the beef and the pork and the vegetables and the chicken.

He ate everything.

Little Miss Splendid used the coming celebration as an excuse to buy a new hat.

A truly splendid red hat!

Little Miss Neat did not think this was very lucky.

What a mess!

Red is the good luck colour for the Chinese New Year and Little Miss Neat made sure there was lots of red in her house.

For extra luck Mr Silly got out the red paint.

And painted the doormat!

And then Mr Wrong hung the lucky Chinese poems …
Upside down!

Which turned out to be the right way up because it was lucky to hang them upside down.

It's not often that Mr Wrong gets something right.

There were lots of things she had to do to make sure that her New Year party went well.

Little Miss Neat had asked her friends to help her decorate her house for New Year.

Little Miss Sunshine put out the flowers.
Little Miss Lucky hung the paper cutouts for happiness.
And Mr Tall hung the lanterns.
High up in the tree.

Very high up!

Little Miss Neat was very busy, very busy cleaning her house.

It was the day before Chinese New Year and this was Little Miss Neat's favourite day of the year.

Spring cleaning day!

She wanted to clean away all last year's bad luck.

And, as we all know, Little Miss Neat loves to clean.

She even vacuumed the walls!

MR. MEN
CHINESE NEW YEAR
Roger Hargreaves

Original concept by
Roger Hargreaves

Written and illustrated by
Adam Hargreaves

EGMONT

MR. MEN   LITTLE MISS

MR. MEN™ LITTLE MISS™ © THOIP (a SANRIO company)

Mr. Men Chinese New Year © 2018 THOIP (a SANRIO company)
Printed and published under licence from Penguin Random House LLC
Published in Great Britain by Egmont UK Limited
The Yellow Building, 1 Nicholas Road, London, W11 4AN

ISBN 978 1 4052 8879 8
68170/002
Printed in Italy

MR. MEN
CHINESE NEW YEAR

Roger Hargreaves